SCIENCE WITH WEATHER

Rebecca Heddle and Paul Shipton

Designed by Sue Grobecker

Illustrated by Kate Davies

Edited by Rebecca Heddle

Consultant: Dave Kennedy BSc, Dip Ed

Contents

Watching the weather

Next time you are outside, look at the weather. It may be sunny or raining, windy or still. Whatever is happening, it can change – sometimes very suddenly. This book will help you find out about weather and how it can change.

Weather diary

Watch the weather every day. You can draw pictures in a weather diary to show what the weather is like.

Does the weather change much from day to day?

Rainy days

When it is raining, but not thundering*, go out with an umbrella. What happens to the rain when it hits the ground?

Can you see any animals or birds? They tend to hide from the rain.

It can rain so hard that it knocks leaves off trees. Sometimes the raindrops are so small you cannot hear them on your umbrella.

Some rain soaks in and makes mud.

Some water lies on the ground as puddles.

2

Do not take shelter under trees when there is thunder and lightning.

Measuring rain

You can make a rain gauge from an empty plastic bottle, and use it to measure how much rain falls each day.

Ask an adult to cut the bottle in half. Stand the top half upside down in the bottom.

This part stops things from falling into the rain you collect.

Stand your rain gauge outside, in the open. Put stones around it to keep it upright.

Use a ruler.

Measure how much water there is in your rain gauge every day, then empty it. Record it in your weather diary.

Try to guess how much water there will be in the rain gauge before you look. There will often be much less than you think.

Forecasting

Scientists study the weather. They learn how it is likely to change, and make forecasts which tell people what it may do.

If you see a weather forecast on television, wait and see how close it is to what happens where you live.

Floods

When it rains very hard for a long time, the water cannot run away. Rivers get much deeper and may overflow.

3

Water in the air

When it rains, some water soaks into the ground, but some is left as puddles. Try this to see what happens to puddles when it stops raining.*

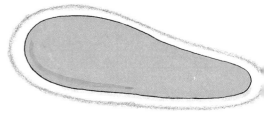

Is the puddle the same size an hour later?

Draw around a puddle with chalk.

It is smaller because some of the water has escaped into the air.

Where the puddle goes

Water in the puddle turns into tiny droplets which are too small to see. The droplets are very light, so they float into the air. This is called evaporation.

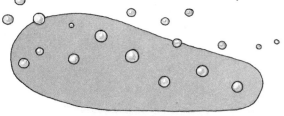

The air is always full of water that has evaporated from rivers, seas and the ground.

Drying out

Wind and warmth make water evaporate more quickly. This is why clothes dry best on windy days when it is warm and sunny.

4   *It will only work if it does not start raining again.

How much water?

You can see how much water there is in the air by looking at pine cones. They open out in dry air, and close up when it is damp.

People say closed pine cones mean rain.

When there is lots of water in the air, it often means that it will rain soon.

Water from the air

Leave a can of drink in the refrigerator overnight. See what happens when you take it out the next day.

The can cools the air around it. Cold air cannot hold as much water. The invisible water droplets in the air join into bigger drops that you can see. This is called condensation.

You can see the drops on the can.

Hot and sticky

Warm air can hold lots of water. The air in tropical places holds so much water that it can make you feel sticky.

Dew

Dew often forms on grass after a warm, dry day. It is water from the air near the ground which condenses as the air cools.

Dew can form on anything near the ground.

Clouds and rain

There is water in your breath. You can see this water as a little cloud when you are out on a cold day.

Tiny water droplets in your breath condense in the cold air (see page 5). They become drops big enough to see, but small enough for the air to hold up.

How clouds form

Air gets cooler as it rises, and the water droplets in it condense and get bigger. The drops of water gather together to make clouds.

The air is colder high up.

Fog

Fog is really a cloud at ground level. Fog that is not very thick is called mist.

Making rain

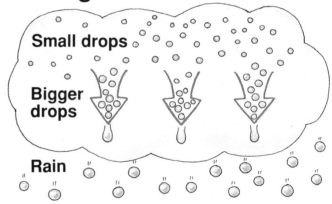

Small drops

Bigger drops

Rain

The drops of water inside a cloud bump into each other and join together. When the drops become too heavy for the air to hold up, they fall as rain.

Up and down

You can make a mini-rainfall in a bowl of hot water. Cover it with plastic food wrap and put ice cubes on top.

Some of the hot water evaporates. It turns into tiny invisible droplets.

The water droplets hit the cold plastic and condense into drops. They join together to make bigger drops. Then they fall back into the water.

Water evaporates from seas, rivers and the soil.

The invisible droplets condense and make clouds.

The water falls back as rain.

The water in the world goes around like this all the time.

Reading clouds

Different types of cloud can bring different sorts of weather. You can forecast what the weather may be like from which clouds you can see coming.

A low blanket of grey clouds can bring light rain.

Dark clouds like this thunder-cloud hold lots of water. They mean it may be stormy.

Small white fluffy clouds usually mean fine weather.

Cold weather

When water gets very cold it freezes and turns into ice. In cold weather the water in ponds, lakes and even rivers can freeze.*

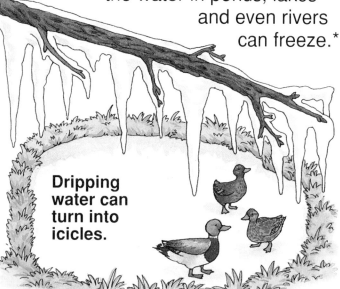

Dripping water can turn into icicles.

Ice power

Fill a plastic bottle with water. Put a coin across the top. Leave it upright in the freezer overnight.

The ice lifts the coin because water gets bigger as it freezes.

Burst pipes

Water pipes can burst if the water inside them freezes and pushes against the sides. Most water pipes are wrapped in thick material to keep out the cold.

Frost

On cold mornings you may see frost on the ground and trees, and on car windows.

You can scrape frost with a stick. It can be so thin that you can melt it by breathing hard on it.

Frost is made up of tiny ice crystals that sparkle.

Sometimes the crystals make patterns.

Never try to walk on frozen ponds or streams.

Snow

When the air is cold enough, water drops in clouds freeze into ice crystals. The crystals stick together to make snowflakes.

You can cool black paper in a freezer and catch snowflakes on it. Look at them with a magnifying glass.

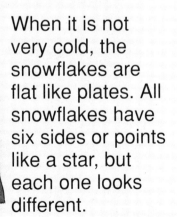

When it is not very cold, the snowflakes are flat like plates. All snowflakes have six sides or points like a star, but each one looks different.

When it is very cold, the snow is powdery. The snowflakes are small and sometimes shaped like needles.

How much snow?

Fill a container with snow. Do not pack it down.

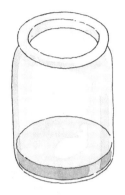

Let the snow melt. How much water was it made of?

Snow takes up much more space than water because there is lots of air inside it.

When you make a snowball or tread on snow, you pack it down and squeeze the air out of it.

Air pushes

We cannot see air, but it is all around us and pushes against everything all the time.

Pushing air trick

Fill a plastic cup to the brim with water.

Put a postcard on top of the cup and push it down.

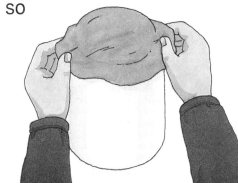

Quickly turn the cup upside down, still holding the postcard in place. Now let go of the postcard.

Do this over the sink.

The postcard stays under the cup because air pushes up against it. Air pushes from underneath things as well as from on top. It pushes so strongly it can keep the water in the cup.

Make a barometer

Sometimes the air pushes harder than at other times. The amount it pushes is called air pressure. Barometers show when the air pressure changes.

You need: empty jar, balloon, rubber band, drinking straw, adhesive tape. cardboard.

Cut the neck off the balloon. Stretch the balloon over the top of the jar. Fasten it tightly with a rubber band so that air cannot get in or out.

Tape one end of the straw to the middle of the balloon. Cut the other end to make a point.

Tape a piece of cardboard to the jar, and mark where the end of the straw points.

If the weather changes, look at your barometer again. Is the straw still pointing at the same place?

The air pressure and the weather in a place often change at the same time.

How the barometer works

The barometer shows when the air pressure outside the jar becomes higher or lower. When it becomes higher, the air pushes down hard on the balloon.

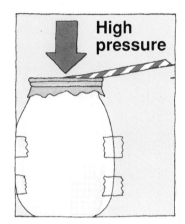

High pressure

The end of the straw points up when the air pushes the balloon down.

When the air pressure is lower, the air inside the jar pushes up on the balloon more than the air outside pushes down.

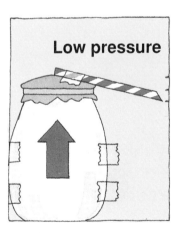

Low pressure

The air pressure is often high when the sky is clear, and low when the weather is cloudy.

Watching wind

You cannot see the wind, but you can see it moving trees, clouds and smoke. Here is something you can make to show how hard the wind is blowing.

Paint one cup and let it dry. Then tape the cups to the edges of the plate.

The cups should all face the same way. →

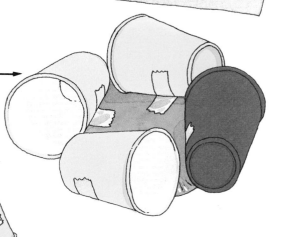

Tape the cotton reel to the middle of the plate, on the other side from the cups.

Push the stick into the ground and slot the cotton reel on top of it.

Bring it in if it starts raining.

The cups catch the wind and spin the plate. Count how many times the painted cup goes around in one minute, and write it in your weather diary.

See how many times the plate spins on different days. The faster the cups go around, the stronger the wind is.

12

*empty spool of thread (US)

Wind directions

Winds are named after the direction they come from – north winds blow from the north. You can make a weather vane to show the direction of the wind.

You need:
stiff cardboard,
knitting needle,
pen top,
adhesive tape,
paper,
compass.

Cut out a cardboard arrow with one wide end and one narrow end, like this.

Tape the pen top to the arrow. Put the pen top on the point of the needle. The arrow should move freely to point at you when you blow at it.

Powerful wind

The strongest winds are called hurricanes. They can break up buildings and knock down trees.

Push the needle through a piece of paper into the ground. Use a compass* to check the directions, and mark the compass points on the paper.

Weigh down the corners with stones.

When the wind blows, the arrow points into the wind. See if the wind often blows from the same direction.

*You could ask an adult to help you use the compass.

13

Moving air

Wind is moving air. When air heats up, it rises. Try these experiments to see how air moves.

Warm air propellor

1. Draw a circle on paper, around a reel of tape. Cut it out and fold it in half twice.

2. Unfold the paper and thread a piece of thin string through it where the folds cross. Knot one end.

3. Cut slits around the edge, to make blades. With the knot on top, bend up one side of each blade so it looks like this.

4. Dangle the propellor over a warm heater*, holding the string. You can see how it swings and twirls.

The heater warms the air above it, so the air rises. It pushes past the propellor's blades and makes it turn.

*Don't let the paper touch the heater.

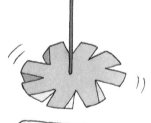

Gliding

Sometimes you can see birds rising without flapping their wings. They are flying in warm air. It pushes them up as it rises.

Warming air

The Sun's heat warms the air in some places more than others. This makes patches of warm air that rise.

14

Making wind

Try this experiment to make a wind. Blow up a balloon and hold the neck shut. Feel the side of the balloon.

You can feel the air pushing out strongly, because it is squashed into the balloon. It is at higher pressure than the air around it.*

Now let the air out of the balloon, holding a hand in front of the neck.

You can feel the air rushing out of the balloon, to even out the pressure. You have made a sort of wind.

Tornadoes

A tornado is a powerful, spinning wind that has very low pressure inside it. It sucks up things in its path, like a huge vacuum cleaner.

Wind always evens out pressure. When warm air rises, it pushes less hard on the things underneath it – the pressure there is lower.

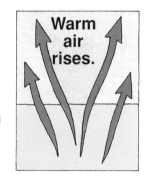

Warm air rises.

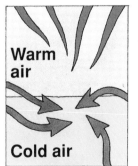

Warm air

Cold air

Cold air moves in from the places around where the pressure is higher. We feel the movement of the air as wind.

*See pages 10–11 for more about air pressure.

15

Heating up

The Earth gets light and heat from the Sun. The Sun is a giant ball of burning gases many times bigger than the Earth.

The Earth is surrounded by a layer of gases called the atmosphere.

The Sun's rays pass through the atmosphere and heat the Earth. Some heat from the Earth goes back into space, but the atmosphere traps some.

Atmosphere

The earth is shaped like a ball.

Sun's rays

Some heat cannot escape.

The way this heat is trapped is called the greenhouse effect. Without it the Earth would be too cold for us to live.

Greenhouse experiment

Put two ice cubes on saucers. Stand a glass over one and put them both in a sunny place.

Look at the ice cubes every five minutes. Which do you think will melt first?

Some heat cannot escape from the glass.

The glass traps some heat, so the ice under it melts first.

Hotter and hotter

Pollution has changed the Earth's atmosphere so it traps more heat. This will probably make the Earth hotter.

Hot and cold

The temperature is how hot or cold the weather is. People measure the temperature with a thermometer. You can make a simple one to see how it works.

Fill a plastic bottle with water. Add some food dye.

Wrap playdough around a clear straw.

Make sure you don't squash the straw.

Put the straw in the bottle, and squash down the playdough so it seals the bottle. This is your thermometer.

Using thermometers

Most thermometers have liquid inside them that gets bigger when the air is warmer. They can show even small changes in temperature.

Look at a thermometer to see how hot it is.

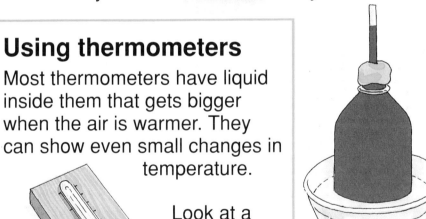

The higher the liquid is, the hotter the day.

Stand your thermometer in a bowl of hot water. Watch what happens to the water in the straw.

Now stand the thermometer in icy water.

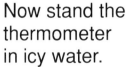

When the water gets hot it takes up more space and moves up the straw. It shrinks again when it cools.

Sun and shadows

Stand in a sunny place in the morning, with your back to the Sun*. Ask a friend to draw around your shadow in chalk.

Do this again in the same place at lunchtime, and in the afternoon. Is your shadow always the same length? Where does it point?

Morning

Midday

Afternoon

Your shadow shows where you block the sunlight.

Your shadow moves, shrinks and grows because the Sun's light comes from different directions through the day.

18

Why shadows change

Stick a straw to a big ball with playdough. Slowly turn the ball in the light of a small lamp. Watch the straw's shadow move.

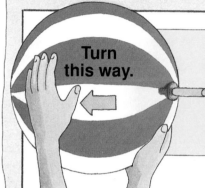

Turn this way.

The shadow is short when the straw points straight at the light.

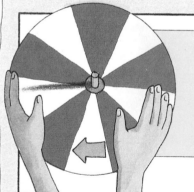

The shadow grows longer as the ball turns and the straw points away.

The Earth turns in the Sun's light once a day. Your shadow changes like the straw's as the light comes from above you or from one side.

*Never look straight at the Sun. It can damage your eyes.

Summer and winter

There are seasons because the Earth tilts like this.

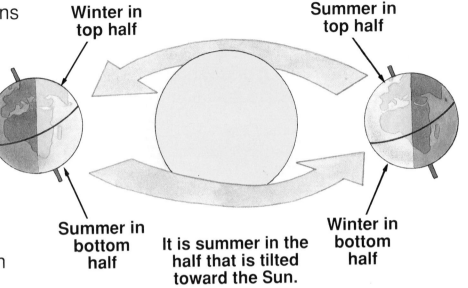

Winter in top half

Summer in top half

Summer in bottom half

It is summer in the half that is tilted toward the Sun.

Winter in bottom half

As well as turning once a day, the Earth moves around the Sun once a year. Because of the way it tilts, different parts of the Earth are closer to the Sun at different times of year.

Hot and cool

Rays of sunlight slant across the half of the Earth that leans away from the Sun. The rays spread out over a large area, so they do not heat it up much.

The Sun's rays shine more directly on the half of the Earth that is tilted toward it. Direct rays make the land hotter.

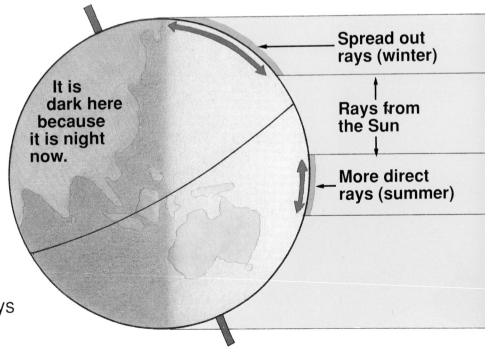

It is dark here because it is night now.

Spread out rays (winter)

Rays from the Sun

More direct rays (summer)

Weather power

Pollution from power stations, factories and cars is harming the world and the air we breathe. Using the Sun's heat and wind power does not cause pollution.

Wind power

You can make a windmill which lifts things when you blow at it and make it turn.

You need:
paper, scissors,
glue,
2 straws,
playdough,
paper clip,
adhesive tape,
thread,
button.

1. Cut out a piece of paper about 10cm (4in) square, and cut slits as shown.

2. Fold the corners marked X into the middle. Glue them down.

3. Make a hole in the middle with a pencil. Push a straw through and squash playdough around it.

It looks like a windmill now.

4. Tape a paper clip to the second straw, like this. Push the windmill straw through the end of the paper clip.

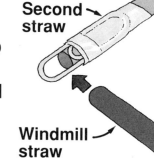

Second straw

Windmill straw

5. Tape some thread to the windmill straw. Tie the button to the thread. Hold the second straw and blow at the windmill.

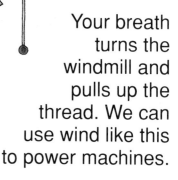

Your breath turns the windmill and pulls up the thread. We can use wind like this to power machines.

Solar water heating

Power from the Sun is called solar power. You can use the heat of the Sun on a summer day to heat water inside a garden hose.

Attach the hose to a tap and turn it on. Turn it off when water comes out of the other end. Stretch a balloon over the end.

The balloon keeps in the water.

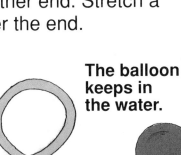

Wind farms

In windy places, people are setting up wind farms. They are fields full of windmills which turn machinery to make electricity.

Stretch out the hose so that it is all lying in the sunshine.

Sunny showers

In very sunny countries, many people have solar water heaters on their roofs. They warm water for baths and showers.

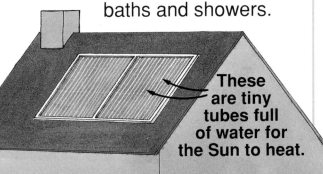

These are tiny tubes full of water for the Sun to heat.

After half an hour, take the balloon off the end and turn on the tap.

The water that comes out first will be hotter than before, until more cold water from the tap comes through. The Sun has heated the water in the hose.

Notes for parents and teachers

These notes will help answer questions that may arise from the activities on earlier pages.

Water in the air (pages 4-5)

Like all substances, water is made up of tiny particles called molecules. They are constantly moving, and often break away and escape. This is evaporation. Heating water makes the molecules move around more quickly, so they break free more easily.

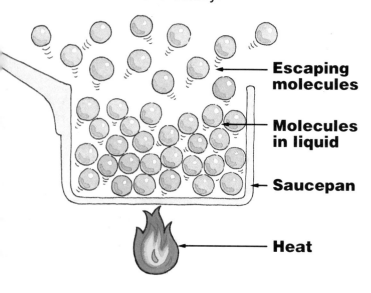

Escaping molecules

Molecules in liquid

Saucepan

Heat

Cooling the molecules makes them move more slowly. This enables them to condense and form a liquid again.

Clouds and rain (pages 6-7)

Although lots of rain comes from the sea, it is never salty. When water evaporates, it leaves behind things that are dissolved in it, like salt.

Cold weather (pages 8-9)

Cooling a liquid makes its molecules slow down even more until they are hardly moving at all. This is when the liquid becomes a solid (freezes). Most liquids grow smaller as they freeze, but water takes up more space, because of the structure of its molecules.

It is possible for the sea to freeze. This usually only happens in polar regions, where it is extremely cold in the winter. It is much more difficult to make the sea freeze because it is salty. Salt water has a lower freezing point than fresh water.

All snowflakes are formed in the same way, by ice crystals sticking to each other. Their patterns are made by the way the snowflakes vibrate as they fall through the air. This is why each one is unique.